Winslow smirked. "It means the time's right to try another love connection," he suggested.

"Hmm . . ." said Cat. "If those two really get together, it would mean no more pounding, no more running, and no more trouble with the Greaser Dogs. It would be a whole new life for CatDog!"

Cat looked over at Dog, who was now fast asleep, with his face in his bowl. "If Shriek and Dog fell in love, there would be no way Cliff and Lube could beat us up. I've got to think of a plan!"

Romancing the Shriek

Romancing the Shriek

by Annie Auerbach, Greg Crosby,
and Lisa Ann Marsoli
illustrated by Gary Johnson

SCHOLASTIC INC.
New York Toronto London Auckland Sydney
Mexico City New Delhi Hong Kong

ROMANCING
the Shriek

Chapter One

It was a beautiful day in Nearburg. The sun was bright and warm. The city streets were buzzing with activity. CatDog was out for their morning stroll. Cat led the way as Dog kept his head high, smelling the air for . . . well, whatever he could smell.

Suddenly they turned a corner and bumped smack into the Greaser Dogs!

"Oops!" said Cat.

"Hey, why don't you look where you're going?" Shriek growled.

"Well, well, well . . . lookee what the dog dragged in," joked Cliff, as he pointed to Cat.

The Greasers surrounded Cat and began to laugh.

"Here for your daily pounding?" Cliff asked CatDog.

Rolling up their sleeves, Shriek and Lube were ready for action.

Zoom! Cat took off with lightning speed, and the chase began. Cat sprang around the corner, down the street, and into an alley in an attempt to ditch the Greasers.

Dog spied an overturned garbage can and jumped into it. "Garbage, garbage, garbage," he chanted happily as Cat tried to catch his breath. "Hey, Cat, want some leftover pizza?"

"That sounds delicious," Cat said sarcastically.

He turned to see Dog's face covered in red tomato sauce. Then Cat burped, and a stinky cloud of pizza breath came out of his mouth.

"Come on, we have to get moving," said Cat impatiently.

Dog frowned. "But we just got here and there's another slice left and . . ."

Three huge shadows fell over CatDog.

Dog looked up and smiled.

"Don't tell me Cliff and the Greasers are standing right behind us," said Cat.

"Okeydokey," Dog replied. "I won't tell you that Cliff and the Greasers are standing right behind us."

Before the Greasers could start pounding, Cat took off! Dog waved good-bye to Cliff and his Greaser pals.

"Stomp ya later!" Cliff barked.

When they had made it home safely, Cat sighed with relief. He leaned against the door, huffing and puffing, and wiped his sweaty brow.

"That was close," wheezed Cat. "Another minute or so and . . ."

"And I could have had a second slice of pizza," Dog added.

"No—we would have *looked* like a slice of pizza!" cried Cat.

"Yeah, that too," Dog agreed.

Winslow appeared in his bathrobe and slippers. "Morning, CatDog," he yawned. "Nice walk?"

"Very funny, rat boy," muttered Cat. "We can't even take a stroll in the neighborhood without those Greaser Dogs ganging up on us. Well, I've had it! I refuse to remain a prisoner in my own house!"

"So what are you going to do?" asked Winslow.

"Can we finish talking in the kitchen?" said Dog. "I'm hungry."

While Dog's head was buried in his bowl of food, Winslow said to Cat, "I got an idea. Did ya ever notice how Shriek always bats those beady little eyes at Dog?"

"Yeah, yeah, yeah," Cat agreed. "We've been through all that. I know Shriek has a thing for Dog. I almost got killed once because of it."

"That's only because you didn't handle it right," Winslow said to Cat. "This time, use your brain, Einstein."

"What's that supposed to mean?" asked Cat.

Winslow smirked. "It means the time's right to try another love connection," he suggested.

"Hmm . . ." said Cat. "If those two really get together, it would mean no more pounding, no more running, and no more trouble with the Greaser Dogs. It would be a whole new life for CatDog!"

Cat looked over at Dog, who was now fast asleep, with his face in his bowl. "If Shriek and Dog fell in love, there would be no way Cliff and Lube could beat us up. I've got to think of a plan!"

Cat thought and thought. Then suddenly he said, "I know! I'll send Shriek a note from Dog inviting her to the movies."

"Now you're thinking, fish breath," said Winslow. "Go on. Knock yourself out!"

Cat wrote the letter while Dog

napped. He wrote one draft after another. Finally, he finished. "This ought to melt that canine's heart . . . if she has one," Cat said to Winslow.

"Heh, heh," laughed Winslow. "I'll even mail it for you, Romeo!"

Everything was set. All Cat had to do was wait until tomorrow night! Soon he would be safe from the Greaser Dogs!

Chapter Two

The next day Shriek checked her mailbox and found the letter that Cat had written for Dog. She sat down on her doggy bed to read it.

Dear Shriek,

You're one dog that's super cool.
When I think of you, I start to drool.
I run around, slobber and pant,
I howl at the moon, I rave and I rant.

My sweet, my love, don't make me moan,
Please say you'll share my stinky bone.
Tonight we'll meet at the movie show,
Be there at eight, in the very first row.

Love,

Your Secret Admirer

Shriek blushed and began fanning herself with the letter. "A secret admirer," she sighed. "Be still my beating heart. But who could it be?" She took a whiff of the letter and almost fainted. "Smells like a hunk o' hound to me!"

Shriek spent the entire day getting ready. She had her nails filed, her fangs brushed, and even took a bath. She could hardly wait for eight o'clock. She ran all the

way to the movie theater, knocking down everyone in her path. When she arrived, Shriek looked up at the marquee. *The Dogfather* was playing. "This must be the place!" she cried.

Shriek cut through the line, pushing everyone out of her way. She was too excited to stop for popcorn or candy.

As she entered the theater, Shriek saw a Saint Bernard in the first row. There was an empty seat next to him.

"What a monstrous mutt!" Shriek thought as she sat down next to him. In no time, he was drooling all over her. "Hey, watch the outfit, bub!" Shriek growled. Then she thought, Could he be my secret admirer? Yuck!

Frightened, the Saint Bernard finally slinked away and found another seat.

"I knew he wasn't the one for me," Shriek said to herself. She looked around, but the lights began to dim. "So where's my secret admirer?" she wondered out loud.

Meanwhile CatDog was running late. A garbage truck had crossed their path on the way to the theater.

"Garbage, garbage, garbage," Dog had chanted.

"No way, Dog," said Cat. "Not tonight. We don't have time for this."

But Dog was already in a trance. He wasn't going to let a garbage truck pass him by.

"Ow, my body, my body!" cried Cat as Dog dragged him along.

When they finally reached the theater, the movie had started.

"You just had to chase that garbage

truck, didn't you?" Cat scolded.

"Sorry, Cat," Dog said, "but I couldn't help myself."

Cat started to walk into the darkened theater when he was snapped back.

"Popcorn, popcorn, popcorn . . ." Dog grunted as he pulled his way up to the snack bar.

"What size would you like?" said the greyhound working behind the counter.

"Hmm . . . what sizes are there?" asked Dog.

"Jumbo, Super Gigantic, and Bigger-than-Texas," the greyhound replied.

"Gee, so many choices . . ." said Dog, his eyes glazing over.

"Come on, Dog!" urged Cat. "We're missing the movie!"

"Okay, I'll take the Bigger-than-Texas

size," said Dog, drooling. "Mmm . . ."

The popcorn was practically bigger than CatDog. Dog held on to it with both paws as Cat dragged him inside the theater.

By now the theater was packed. In the dark, Cat checked the front row, and only one seat was available. It was next to Shriek.

What luck! Cat thought as they quickly made their way over.

CatDog sat down. Then suddenly they heard a familiar voice.

"Yo, Shriek. Fancy meetin' you here," the voice said.

"Cliff," Shriek said, looking over, "what are you doing here?"

"Shh!" said a few other dogs in the theater.

"Dis is my favorite picture. I've seen it twenty-seven times," said Cliff.

"Uh . . . yeah, mine, too," added Lube, as he and Cliff made their way over to Shriek.

"Lube, you've never seen dis one before," Cliff pointed out.

"Uh . . . der . . . what does dat have to do with it?" answered Lube.

"Down in front!" shouted an angry dog.

Lube and Cliff tried to sit in what they thought was an empty seat.

Suddenly everything went dark for CatDog!

Chapter Three

CatDog found themselves crushed by an enormous weight. Popcorn flew everywhere!

"It's so dark in here, I can barely see my paw in front of my face," said Cliff. "Lucky for me I got da last empty seat in da ferst row. And right next to Shriek, too."

"Uh, *I* got da seat," said Lube, trying to squeeze in.

"No, bonehead, I was here ferst," replied Cliff.

It was clear that Cliff and Lube didn't

know they were sitting on CatDog. They were too busy fighting over the seat.

CatDog could hardly breathe. And Cat was feeling the weight of Cliff the most.

A horrible thought crossed Shriek's mind. Could Cliff be her secret admirer? "Uh . . . Cliff, h-have you been writin' any poetry lately?" she whispered.

"Poe-a-tree?" Cliff asked. "What kinda tree is dat?"

"Never mind," Shriek said, relieved. She realized that Cliff couldn't spell love, let alone feel it.

The coming attractions were over and the movie finally began.

"Boy, dose are big dogs, huh, Cliff?" Lube said in awe.

"Yeah," Cliff agreed. "I never sat in da ferst row before."

"There's only room for one of us, you greasy mutt," said the Doberman on the screen.

"Hey, who you callin' a greasy mutt?" yelled Lube.

Shriek sighed. Then she took another look around for any dog that might be her secret admirer. No dog seemed to fit the bill. Shriek asked the other Greasers, "Would you guys mind movin' to some other seat? Maybe two of them?"

"Huh?" said Lube.

"What for?" Cliff asked.

"Uh . . . I kinda like to spread out when I watch a movie," she explained. Shriek couldn't let Cliff or Lube know about her secret admirer. "Just go sit somewhere else, okay?"

"Yes, yes, yes. Please go sit somewhere

else," Cat whispered. He was becoming as flat as a pancake.

"You know there ain't no other place to sit!" Cliff said at the top of his voice. "Dis joint is packed!"

"Yeah," Lube agreed. "Like a can of sardines."

The audience was getting annoyed at all the commotion. They started to hiss at the Greaser Dogs.

"All of youse butt out!" Cliff shouted back to the crowd. "Dis here is a private argument!"

Meanwhile Cat knew he had to do something drastic. He opened his mouth and bit down hard on the fat, greasy blob above him.

"YEOWW!" shrieked Cliff as he went straight up in the air.

Lube was thrown sideways.

CatDog managed to slide off the seat and onto the floor before Cliff came back down.

Finally an usher came and tossed Shriek and the Greaser Dogs out of the theater.

"Hey, watch it, buddy!" Shriek yelled at the usher.

Cat crawled under the seats, making his way slowly toward the exit, as Dog inhaled all the food scraps on the floor.

As CatDog left the theater, Cat spotted Shriek, Cliff, and Lube.

Shriek looked really mad as she shadowboxed. "I'm gonna brain that moronic mongrel if he shows up," she mumbled to herself.

"Uh, gotta go!" Cat said under his

breath and quickly led Dog the other way.

"Well, that was a total flop," Cat wheezed as they made their way home.

"Not a total flop, Cat," said Dog, licking his lips. "That theater has the best snacks!"

Chapter Four

The next day Cat was determined to come up with another plan to get Dog and Shriek together.

He looked in the newspaper. Suddenly Cat saw it—an ad that would help him play cupid. An ad that would bring an end to his life as the Greasers' punching bag. An ad that would change everything!

Everyone loves the circus!
COME SEE THE DINGLING BROS. CIRCUS
ONE DAY ONLY!
SPECIAL 2-FOR-1 DISCOUNT!

Dog was eating, as usual, when Winslow walked into the kitchen. "Hey, Cat," he said, "whatcha readin'?"

"All about my perfect future," Cat answered, as a plan began to form in his head.

"Then you must be reading the comics," joked Winslow. "'Cause *that's* funny."

"I've got a plan that can't miss," said Cat.

"Well, since the last plan went so well, I can't wait to hear the new one," Winslow said sarcastically.

Cat glared at him. "This time I'll invite Shriek to meet her secret admirer at the circus."

"Everyone loves the circus," Winslow said.

"I love the circus!" said Dog looking up from his food. Circus was the only word he'd heard.

"I rest my case," Winslow said, as Dog went back to devouring his food.

"This time, though," Cat continued, "I have got to make sure Shriek won't mistake someone else for her secret admirer."

"What do you want?" asked Winslow. "A neon sign?"

"Very funny, rodent," said Cat. "But that does give me an idea. . . ."

By that afternoon there was another letter in Shriek's mailbox.

"Oh, no, not again," Shriek whined. "If this mutt is toying with my heart—I'll teach him a lesson!"

But she couldn't resist. She opened the letter and read it.

Dear Shriek,

I missed you at the movie show,
But I still dig ya, don't ya know.
This time, to meet me face to face,
I've come up with the perfect place.
If you like this note I sent,
Please meet me in the circus tent.
Under a balloon that's red,
You'll find my doggone handsome head.

Love,
Your Secret Admirer

"I hate the stupid circus!" Shriek shrieked.

Then her heart got the better of her. "Well, maybe I should give love one more try. . . ."

Chapter Five

Dog was so excited. He couldn't wait to get to the circus! "Are you ready, Cat?" asked Dog impatiently. "Huh? Are you? Are you?"

"Yup," replied Cat. "Let's go. We just have to make one little stop along the way."

"At Taco Depot?" Dog asked excitedly.

"Not today, Dog," Cat replied. "But how about if I buy you a big, red balloon instead?"

"Hi-ho diggety!" answered Dog.

And with that CatDog set off.

Winslow went along, too. He wanted to see how Cat's plan would backfire this time.

When they got to the balloon store, Dog was in doggy heaven. All the big and brightly colored balloons reminded him of balls, which he loved to chase.

"Okay, how about this one?" suggested Cat. But there was no reply. "Dog? Dog?"

"Hiya, Cat!" called Dog in a squeaky voice.

Cat turned around. Dog's head was inflated. It seemed that he had been sipping a little helium. Actually, it was *a lot* of helium. Dog was even floating off the ground!

"Gee, Dog, you're looking a little light-headed!" said Winslow. "Heh! Heh!"

Dog stifled a laugh, which caused a large burst of helium to come out of Cat's mouth. It nearly blew over the clerk working behind the counter.

"Oops. Sorry," squeaked Cat. "Uh, we'll just take the red one." He paid the clerk, then he, Dog, and Winslow headed for the circus.

Once inside the big top, Cat's heart sank. He looked around the arena and saw hundreds of big red balloons in the audience.

"Heh! Heh! Good plan, Cat!" joked Winslow.

"Shut up, blue boy," answered Cat.

Dejected, Cat led them to their seats.

Meanwhile Shriek was walking along the center ring looking for her secret admirer in the audience. "What a stupid mutt!" she hissed. "There are so many red balloons here, how am I supposed to know who is in love with me?"

Suddenly a clown on a unicycle rode by and grabbed Shriek.

"Hey, look what I found!" the clown shouted to the ringmaster. "An escapee from the dog act!"

"What? Why, I'll pulverize you, you crazy clown!" Shriek screamed. "Boy, I hate the stupid circus!"

But the clown didn't let Shriek go.

"If you don't put me down, clown face, I'm gonna feed you a knuckle sandwich!" Shriek threatened.

As the clown rode across the ring, Mr. Sunshine, the trapeze artist, swung into action. He grabbed Shriek from the clown's shoulders and threw her to his partner on the other trapeze.

In the stands Dog was munching on

caramel corn while Cat looked around for Shriek. "I must have been nuts to think that we'd ever find her in a crowd like this," Cat sighed.

"You said it, I didn't," snickered Winslow.

"Hey, lookee what we have here!" a voice called. "I bet you feel right at home in the circus!"

Cat looked up to see Cliff and Lube towering over them.

"And youse in our seats," continued Cliff.

"Uh . . . yeah," Lube added. "And our seats should be in dose seats."

"You must be mistaken," replied Cat. "The greasy section is on the other side of the ring."

Just then Dog shouted, "Hey, isn't that

Shriek on the flying trapeze? I didn't know she could do stuff like that! Cool!"

Shriek somersaulted through the air between the two acrobats, screaming in terror.

Cat turned around to look. "Shriek? Where?"

"Look!" said Dog, pointing.

"Oh, no!" Cat cried.

"Now *that's* funny!" Winslow said.

"What's she doin'?" asked Cliff.

"Dog, this is your big chance to be a hero. We gotta save her!" Cat said. "Let's go!"

"Where do you think you're going?" yelled Cliff. "Come on, Lube, let's get 'em!"

Lube and Cliff chased Cat as he started running toward the center ring. Just then, Mr. Sunshine lost his grip on Shriek. Shriek

missed the net and down she went. Cat looked up and saw Shriek falling toward him.

Then everything went black!

Winslow couldn't help laughing. "Now, that's what I call a circus act! Heh! Heh!"

Chapter Six

The next thing Cat knew, he was back home with an ice pack on his head. Dog was sleeping, sucking caramel popcorn from his teeth between snores.

"Dog, wake up! What happened?" Cat asked.

Dog opened his eyes and smiled at Cat sleepily.

"Well, when I woke up," Dog began, "they were taking Shriek to the hospital. She was still knocked out. You were out, too,

but you were talking in your sleep. You kept saying how you hated the stupid circus. Anyway, I was gettin' awful hungry so I dragged us home, put an ice pack on your head, and I ate dinner . . . for both of us."

"So, just how long have I been out?" asked Cat.

"Three—" Dog began.

"Wow, three hours is a long time," sighed Cat.

"Three days," Dog finished.

Meanwhile Winslow was behind closed doors with an envelope. It was addressed to Cat. He held it up to the light, but couldn't see what it was. Next, he brought out a tiny iron and tried to steam it open. Finally, he gave up and walked into the living room.

"Good morning, Sleeping Beauty,"

Winslow said. "That was some cat nap you took."

"Don't bother me now, Winslow. We've got to get to the hospital right away," said Cat, tossing the ice pack aside.

"Why, Cat?" asked Dog. "You still not feelin' well?"

"Not me," Cat explained. "I've never felt better in my life!"

A new plan had begun to form in Cat's head. We've got to see Shriek and let her know that it was Dog who broke her fall and saved her life, he thought. He'll be a hero! She'll love him forever! And I'll never be pounded by those Greasers again!

"Hey, Cat," Winslow said, holding out the soggy envelope. "This letter came for you while you were . . . er, out."

Cat stopped. "Huh? Oh." He grabbed

it out of Winslow's hands.

"Why is it all wet?" asked Cat.

"Uh . . . it fell into Dog's water bowl," Winslow lied.

"Hmm . . ." said Cat, smelling the letter. Then he began to read.

Dear Cat,

**You've got the whiskers
   I long to touch,
You've got the fur
   that I love so much.
You're a giant among cats,
   a feline supreme.**

The number one cat,
    a kitty-cat dream.
You're everything I've wished
    for and more,
Please meet me at eight, dear,
behind the fish store.

Love,

Your Secret Admirer

Chapter Seven

A silly, sloppy look came over Cat's face as he melted into the couch.

"Wait a minute. Now *I've* got a secret admirer?" Cat said dreamily. "Be still my beating heart."

Dog couldn't believe his eyes. He'd never seen Cat behave this way.

"What about going to visit Shriek in the hospital, Cat?" Dog said. "Shouldn't we be going? Yoo-hoo! Cat?"

"Going? Yes, I must be going," Cat

said, as if in a trance. "It's nearly eight and I have a date. I mustn't be late."

"Man, that is one screwball feline," Winslow observed.

With that, Cat floated out the door dragging poor, confused Dog behind him. They made their way through town until they reached the fish store. It was nearly eight o'clock.

"Just think, Dog, in a matter of moments I will meet my secret admirer," sighed Cat, looking off into space.

"Uh, yeah," replied Dog warily.

Turning the corner, Cat took them down the dark side alley and to the back of the store.

When they got there, they stopped and waited. Dog took the opportunity to investigate a garbage can while Cat gazed

dreamily at the full moon.

Just then three familiar shadows fell over CatDog.

Cat gulped. "Greaser Dogs?" he asked hesitantly.

"Right you are!" Cliff mocked gleefully.

Shriek moved in closer to Cat and said, "You've got the whiskers I long to touch. You've got the fur that I love so much."

"M-my secret admirer?" gulped Cat.

"Hey," Shriek said, "if you can be mine, I can be yours, can't I?"

"But, but, but . . . yeah, well," Cat sputtered.

"I was lyin' in the hospital bed thinkin'," began Shriek, "and I remembered that when I got thrown out of the movies the other day, I noticed you two crawlin' out of the theater."

"Uh-oh," Cat said to himself.

"And then I landed right on top of you at the circus," Shriek continued. "It seemed strange that both times when I was supposed to meet my so-called 'secret admirer,' you morons were around. So I put one and one together and got CatDog."

"How did you know it was me?" asked Cat fearfully.

"There was a faint scent of whitefish chub on the last note," replied Shriek.

"Hmm . . . isn't that interesting?" Cat laughed nervously.

"Not half as interesting as what comes next," said Cliff.

"Der . . . what comes next?" Lube asked.

"The pounding!" cried Shriek.

Cat turned to Dog. "You know, I've got a *new* plan . . . RUN!"

About the Authors

Annie Auerbach is a children's book editor for a Los Angeles publishing company. She is also a freelance writer. Just like Cat, she hates spicy food, and just like Dog, she loves new adventures.

Greg Crosby, a writer and cartoonist for many years at the Walt Disney Company, has written dozens of children's storybooks, graphic novels, and comic strips. He lives in Sherman Oaks, California, with his wife and their 180-pound golden retriever, Moose.

Lisa Ann Marsoli is the author of over 100 books for children. She is the co-owner of a book packaging company in Los Angeles. Her significant others include one husband, one child, and one cat.

Hi-ho diggety! Here's a sneak peek at Chapter Book #2 in the CatDog series. You'LL flip over this double-header. . . .

Cat's Big Night

"What are you, nuts?" Winslow interrupted. "You're not going to the party. The invitation is addressed to Cat. Just Cat. And look at what it says down here—'no children or dogs allowed.' Well, that leaves you out!"

Cat stopped and looked at his other half. Dog cocked his head and looked back at Cat. Cat frowned. Cat knew there was no way he could go to the party. Unless . . .

"Well, there is one way . . ." Cat began.

FLIP THIS BOOK OVER! 2 STORIES IN 1!

Dog Behind Bars

"Please, please, please, Winslow," Dog begged. "Please show me what you have behind your back."

Winslow smiled a sneaky smile. He knew he was causing trouble for Cat. And causing trouble for Cat was Winslow's favorite hobby. "Well, if you insist," he said. He held a bright yellow ball right out in front Dog's face.

Dog's eyes popped wide open. "Ball . . ." said Dog in a hypnotic trance.

FLIP THIS
BOOK OVER!
2 STORIES
IN 1!